MEET ALL THESE FRIENDS IN
BUZZ BOOKS:

Thomas the Tank Engine

The Wind in the Willows

The Animals of Farthing Wood

Skeleton Warriors

Fireman Sam

First published in Great Britain 1996 by Buzz Books
an imprint of Reed International Books
Michelin House, 81 Fulham Road, London SW3 6RB
and Auckland, Melbourne, Singapore and Toronto

Puppy In My Pocket™ © 1994 Morrison Entertainment Group Inc.
Licensed by Just Licensing Limited
Illustrations by Arkadia, copyright © 1996 Reed International Books
Text copyright © 1996 Reed International Books

ISBN 1 85591 550 2

Printed in Italy by Olivotto

PUPPY
IN MY POCKET ™

The Perfect Puppy Party

Story by Susan Allan

Illustrations by Arkadia

buzz books

All the puppies were having a well-deserved rest at the Pocketville Hotel.

Zsa Zsa was relaxing on a cushion, taking care not to ruffle her newly clipped fur. Wellington and Dixie were having great fun playing on the bone slide, and Dotty and Stuart were watching a Puppy Game Show on the television.

Dotty turned to her friend. "I wish I could

take part in this quiz," she said. "The top prize is wonderful – you can win a year's supply of puppy food and all the toys you can carry."

"It would be nice," replied Stuart, "but we don't exactly need it." He trotted over to the window and looked out across the road at the Pocketville Hospital opposite.

Dotty came over to join him and looked
out. Through the window of the hospital
they could see poor puppy patients tucked
up in their beds. One little puppy had his
paw in a bandage and another had a big
plaster on his head. They all looked sad
and miserable.

"They are the ones that could really do with cheering up," said Stuart.

Dotty thought hard.

"You're right you know," she replied. "And I think I've got an idea to help them out."

"Listen-up puppies," Dotty called.

All the puppies stopped what they were doing and huddled round her.

"I know that we're having a nice time," she continued, "but Stuart has put an idea into my head. I think it's time we helped out some other puppies less fortunate than ourselves."

Most of the puppies nodded in agreement, but a few of them groaned.

"We haven't had a holiday for ages," said Zsa Zsa. "Can't we just enjoy ourselves for a change?"

"Take a look out of that window," scolded Dotty, "and I think you'll change your mind."

Zsa Zsa and some of the other puppies went to the window to look out.

They saw the hospital and all the unhappy puppies inside.

"I'm sorry," said Zsa Zsa. "That was very selfish of me. But what can we do to help?"

Dotty looked at her friends.

"How about a party?" she suggested. "Those poor little puppies need to be cheered up and I think a party would do the trick."

"I'll organise the entertainment," volunteered Stuart.

"And I'll find some decorations," said Zsa Zsa.

"What will you do, Dotty?" asked Wellington.

Dotty looked at her friends. "Now, that's a secret," she said mysteriously, and walked off.

The next few days were a busy time for the puppies involved in the surprise party.

Zsa Zsa visited all the local shop-keepers and persuaded them to give her old paper, paints, card and glue. She rushed back home and made some decorations.

Wellington visited her to see how she was doing.

"You're busy, Zsa Zsa," he said, seeing the mess strewn around her.

"Yes," she replied proudly. "And look what I've made." She showed him the beautiful banners and streamers she had created to decorate the hospital.

GET WELL

"I've even made a party hat for each guest," she explained. She looked at her friend and had an idea. "Now you're here Wellington, you can help me blow up the balloons," she laughed.

Stuart, who always wanted to
be a performer, decided to provide
the entertainment himself.

He gathered together Maggie's beagle
babies and practised his jokes and tricks
on them.

"And now you will see my finest trick,"
he announced in a grand voice. "Watch
closely as I make this toy disappear!"

The beagle babies gasped in awe as Stuart covered the toy with a handkerchief, and whispered the secret magic words.

He lifted the handkerchief to reveal . . . the toy!

All the beagle babies giggled.

"I think you need a bit more practice, Stuart," sniggered one.

"Perhaps I'll stick to jokes," muttered Stuart as he ambled off.

Meanwhile, Dixie was visiting all her friends and persuading them to bake cakes for the party.

"It's to help the sick puppies at the Pocketville hospital," she explained. "We're going to hold a surprise party to cheer them up."

Soon Dixie had enough cake to feed almost every puppy in Pocketville!

"I think I've got enough food now," she said looking at the enormous spread in front of her.

But she didn't notice one naughty puppy who had decided to taste a cake a little too early!

Back at the hospital, puppy patients gazed
out of the windows sadly.

"Look at Zsa Zsa with all those balloons,"
sighed Charlie. "It looks like there is going
to be a big party in Pocketville soon."

"Yes," replied Bertie who had the measles. "I wish we weren't missing it."

But it was time for their medicine again, and the puppies had to be tucked up in bed for a snooze.

At last all the preparations were complete and the kindly puppies were ready to hold their surprise party.

Stuart called his helpers together. "Are you all ready?" he asked.

A cheer went up.

"Gather together everything we need and we'll go to the hospital now."

The puppies busily packed the cakes, streamers and balloons when suddenly Wellington asked: "But where is Dotty?"

The puppies shook their heads.

"We can't have the party without her. It was her idea after all," said Wellington.

"Don't worry about Dotty," said Stuart. "I'm sure she'll find a way of surprising us."

Later that day when the party had finished, the puppies were at the hospital clearing up. "I think the party was a success," said Dixie as she looked at all the smiling faces.

Zsa Zsa's hats were very popular, and Charlie wouldn't take his off even though the party had ended.

Bertie asked Stuart to teach him some tricks and every puppy in the hospital had tasted some of Dixie's delicious cakes.

But still Dotty didn't appear.

"Oh well," sighed Wellington, "we can tell her all about it tomorrow. But now, puppies; the nurse tells me it's nearly time for all of you to go to bed."

The puppy patients groaned.

"We're always allowed to watch a few minutes of television before bedtime," they pleaded.

"All right then," said Stuart as he turned on the set.

There was a huge gasp of surprise as all the puppies looked at the screen. There was Dotty and she was taking part in the Puppy Game Show.

It was the final question, and the scores were level.

"Name a member of Pocketville's most popular dog-band, the Doggy Duo," asked the host.

The first entrant answered, "Prince."

"Incorrect!" said the host. "Now here's a chance for competitor number two," he continued.

The second entrant answered.

"Incorrect!" said the host.

Now it was Dotty's turn. She answered hesitantly: "Is it Ringo?" she asked.

There was a pause that seemed to last for ages.

The Game Show host turned to Dotty,
took a breath, and then said:

"Correct!"

All the puppy patients turned to each
other and looked in disbelief.

"You have won our star prize of the
evening," continued the Game Show host.
"– a year's supply of puppy food and as
many toys as you can take home!"

Dotty jumped around with glee, and then said: "Thank you so much. I'm very pleased to have won this prize because I've won it for some very special puppies. I would like to donate my prize to the puppies in the Pocketville hospital! They have had a party today, and I wanted to give them a special gift."

Back at the hospital all the puppies cheered and laughed.

"I told you that Dotty would do something to surprise us!" giggled Stuart.